Animals

Dolphins

by Nick Rebman

FOCUS READERS

FOCUS READERS

www.focusreaders.com

Focus Readers is distributed by North Star Editions:
sales@northstareditions.com | 888-417-0195

Produced for Focus Readers by Red Line Editorial.

Photographs ©: Irina No/Shutterstock Images, cover, 1; Andrea Izzotti/Shutterstock Images, 4, 7, 15, 16 (top left), 16 (bottom left); Willyam Bradberry/Shutterstock Images, 9; timsimages/Shutterstock Images, 11, 16 (top right); IanCale/iStockphoto, 13; Jag_cz/ Shutterstock Images, 16 (bottom right)

ISBN
978-1-63517-848-7 (hardcover)
978-1-63517-949-1 (paperback)
978-1-64185-152-7 (ebook pdf)
978-1-64185-051-3 (hosted ebook)

Library of Congress Control Number: 2018931096

Printed in the United States of America
Mankato, MN
May, 2018

About the Author

Nick Rebman enjoys reading, drawing, and traveling to places where he doesn't speak the language. He lives in Minnesota.

Table of Contents

Dolphins

Dolphins live in the **sea**.

Dolphins can swim.

A dolphin has **flippers**.

A dolphin has a **fin**.

A dolphin has a tail.

These parts help the dolphin swim.

fin
tail
flipper

Behavior

Dolphins swim fast.

Dolphins can jump.

Dolphins like to play.

Dolphins live in groups.
The groups are
called **pods**.
The pod stays together.
The pod looks for food.

Food

Dolphins eat fish.

Dolphins do not chew.

They eat the fish whole.

Dolphins are smart.
Dolphins can live for
40 years.

Glossary

fin

pods

flippers

sea

Index